Love Rewound

A BBF, SMALL TOWN, SLOW BURN, SECOND CHANCE ROMANCE

CORAL COVE
BOOK FIVE

JAX WILDER

Love Rewound

CORAL COVE SERIES

Jax Wilder

RAINBOW QUARTZ PUBLISHING

Love Rewound © 2024 by Jax Wilder

Published by Rainbow Quartz Publishing

Edmonds WA, 98026

ISBN: 978-1-961714-47-2

First Edition: 2024

Cover design by Miranda Townsend

Interior design by Miranda Townsend

For permissions or inquiries, please contact:

Rainbow Quartz Publishing

rainbowquartzpublishing@gmail.com

For Pattie

ONE

Amelia

Rewind Rentals was the last beacon of a bygone era in a world dominated by streaming services. The smell of aged vinyl and old VHS tapes greeted me as I stepped inside, a comforting reminder of the countless hours I'd spent here. This store was the place where the past wasn't just preserved—it was celebrated. We were one of the last video rental stores left, and I'd done everything I could to keep the doors open.

"Good morning, Amelia," Mia Jenkins called, the bell above the door jingling merrily as she entered. She came like clockwork, swapping her returns for fresh titles. She was always ready to chat about her favorite old movies and her love of monster movies in particular. The girl was a sucker for anything wolf-like.

"Good morning, Mia. Looking for anything special today?" I asked, sliding behind the counter.

"Just browsing," she said with a smile. "But you know I always welcome a recommendation if you have one."

"Well, that's good because I have two for you." I held up the first film. "*Wolves* came out in 2014 and is a lesser-known

1

Jason Momoa film. He plays a werewolf wandering the Canadian countryside. It's sexy AF."

"Sold," Mia said, snagging the film from me and appraising the back cover. "It sounds good, right up my alley."

"The other is *The Howling Two: Your Sister is a Werewolf*." I beamed at her.

"They made a part two? Oh my gosh, that's amazing. Yes, to both, please!" Mia said with a toothy grin.

Posters of classic films lined the walls, and shelves were filled with VHS tapes, DVDs, vinyl records, and rare movie memorabilia. It was a place out of time, a haven for those who, like me, clung to the tangible magic of physical media. Sure, it was a little outdated, but it was home.

The door chimed again, and this time it was Mr. Gorman, another regular. "Amelia, do you have that new shipment of 80s horror flicks?"

"Right over here," I said, leading him to a display I'd set up yesterday. "We have classics like *The Shining*, *Nightmare on Elm Street*, and *Child's Play*. But we also have some more eclectic titles like *Popcorn*, *From Beyond*, and *Pieces*. I'm sure you'll find a few in there you might like."

He grinned, eyes lighting up. "You always know just what I need."

Moments like these reminded me why I fought so hard to keep this place open. My parents thought I was crazy, holding onto this relic from the past when everything was going digital. They wanted to sell the store and retire, but I couldn't let that happen. Rewind Rentals was more than a business. It was a piece of our family's legacy.

My phone buzzed.

> Jake: Hey, can we talk? Got someone I want you to meet.

I frowned, wondering what he wanted. He only seemed to show up when there was a crisis because he wrecked his car or apartment or whatever accident he'd found himself in that day. But he was my brother, and I owed him at least a conversation.

Me: Sure, come by the store.

Jake: Groovy, I'll see you in an hour.

Four hours later than he said he'd be by, the door chimed, and I looked up to see Jake walking in with a tall, dark-haired man.

My heart skipped a beat as Flynn Callahan walked through the door. His presence filled the room, and made my pulse quicken. I tried to focus on the stack of tapes in front of me, but the heat rising in my cheeks betrayed me. As he approached, the familiar scent of him—earthy, masculine—wrapped around me, weaving through me, stirring memories I thought I had long buried.

"Amelia," he greeted me, his voice lower than I remembered. It was the kind of voice that made my stomach flip. I looked up, meeting his gaze, and for a moment, the air between us seemed to thicken, charged with something unspoken. His eyes lingered on my lips before flicking back to meet mine, making me acutely aware of every inch of space between us.

I hadn't seen Flynn in literal years, not since he graduated and moved away. Not since he and… I pushed the thought away. The past was the past, and it could stay that way. I didn't need Sexy-Mc-Look-At-Me-I'm-Flynn-And-I-Do-What-I-Want coming back and messing up my life again.

I got over him, dammit.

"Amelia, you remember Flynn," Jake said with a mischievous glint in his eyes.

3

"Of course," I said, trying to keep my voice steady. Flynn looked different somehow—more mature, confident. And annoyingly handsome. Fuck. "How could I forget?"

"Hey, Ams," Flynn said, offering a smile that could melt ice in Antarctica.

My knees threatened to buckle. "How long have you been back in town?" I asked, not entirely sure if I wanted to hear the answer.

"A few days ago," he said casually.

I had overheard someone mention a Callahan was back in town, but I didn't allow myself to believe, even for a moment, that it could be Flynn. "I didn't realize you'd made plans to move back."

"It was a recent decision. Life's funny like that sometimes. You know?"

No, I didn't know. And I wasn't about to let him charm his way back into my life. He had broken my heart once, and he didn't get to just walk in here and act like nothing had changed. Things that shouldn't matter right now: the way Flynn smells like home; the sudden, irrational urge to jump over the counter, run my fingers through his hair, and close the distance between us.

I tilted my head, forcing a calmness I didn't feel. "No, I don't. Please, enlighten me."

Flynn looked at Jake, who only shrugged his shoulders and silently exchanged an entire conversation between them. I could only guess at what.

"Jake told me that your parents were thinking of retiring and that you wanted to keep the store open. He mentioned you might need some help around this place," Flynn said, taking in the state of the store. "It looks exactly the same as the day I left town."

Flashes of that painful day attempted to claw their way out of the dark hole I'd buried them in. Like the queen I was, I kicked them back down.

He left, and I stayed. That's all there was to it.

"I wanted to lend my services, for old time's sake," Flynn said.

I forced a smile, my mind racing. The last thing I needed was Flynn swooping in and offering his unsolicited advice. But the look on Jake's face told me he was serious about the request.

"Help would be great," I started, more to Jake than Flynn. "But I can manage just fine."

Jake rolled his eyes. "Come on, Ams. I know you could use the extra pair of hands, or you wouldn't be begging me for help."

"I'm not begging you for help. I wanted you to have an opinion about the future of Rewind Rentals. Not for you to pawn your friends off on me to get out of having an opinion. Those are two different things, Jake."

Flynn cleared his throat. "In my current line of work, I specialize in assisting struggling small businesses like yours in transforming their financial statements from losses to profits."

I shot daggers at Jake. "That's family business. Jake had no business—"

Jake cut me off. "Can we just have a quick chat? Alone."

I let out a sigh and gave him a curt nod. We walked out of earshot of Flynn.

"Look," Jake said, his voice tinged with frustration, "I know exactly what you asked, but I'm afraid I don't have the answers. When I don't know the answers, I trust the people who do. I prefer to stay in my lane. Flynn is good at this stuff. If you want to save Rewind Rentals, this is the best way I know how."

I shot a quick glance at Flynn. "He's never worked here. Am I supposed to just divulge private information to this guy?"

"He's not just some guy, Amelia, and you know it. Flynn

is practically my brother. Besides, it's not like we have a lot of other options right now. If we don't make some changes, we're going to lose this place. We can't live in the red forever."

"It's not that bad yet," I said, but I didn't believe my own words.

"Can you please give it a shot?"

"We can't afford the help."

Jake spun on his heels. "She can't afford a consultant, Flynn."

"No worries. When I turn this place around," Flynn said with a wink. "Not if, but when I turn this place around, the local acknowledgment alone will garner me the respect and word of mouth I'll need to start my firm right here, based in Coral Cove."

"Seems to me he's as cheap as they get." Jake grinned.

My eyes narrowed at Flynn. "Unless you have practical experience in a rental business of this kind, I won't consider your advice on how to change my business. If we can turn a profit, I'll pay you for your services."

"When you turn a profit," Flynn corrected with a grin that could only be described as immoral.

I rolled my eyes. "Fine. When?"

"How about now?"

In such close proximity to Flynn, I could feel the tension between us intensifying. There was history with Flynn. He wasn't just my brother's best friend. He was a mistake, and I needed to stay focused on saving the store. I couldn't afford to get distracted by someone like Flynn, no matter how charming he was.

TWO

Moving back to Coral Cove was the last thing I thought I'd be doing. But there I was, standing in the middle of Rewind Rentals—a time capsule of my childhood. The familiar scent of old popcorn butter and a subtle plastic funk wafted through the air, triggering a rush of forgotten memories. I could almost hear the laughter and feel the excitement as Jake, Amelia, and I perused the shelves, searching for the perfect movie.

Oh, Amelia.

It was a physical blow seeing her again after all these years. She always had this aura about her, the warmth of a wildfire spirit and a drive that drew people in and refused to be put out. But today, the weariness in her eyes and the heaviness in her voice betrayed the immense pressure of trying to keep this place running. I wanted to help. Not just because Jake asked, but because I could see how much this meant to her. After all this time, it was still Amelia.

"Okay, buddy," Jake said, breaking my reverie. "You ready to get to work?"

"Absolutely," I said, rolling up my sleeves. "What's first on the agenda?"

Amelia gave me a wary look, as if she was still deciding whether she could trust me. She bit her lip while she thought. I wanted to bite that lip.

"We need to reorganize the inventory," she said. "Customers have been complaining that they can't find what they're looking for."

"Got it," I said, moving toward the shelves to assess the situation. "So, you're currently organized by…" I trailed off, unsure of exactly what the organization system was.

"By year first and then by genre," Amelia said proudly. "Unfortunately, the previous part-time assistant could not successfully understand and use the filing system. The folks didn't notice right away, which resulted in this. Nothing is where it should be."

My eyes narrowed, trying to find the right way not to insult her in the first five minutes of my first shift. "Okay, we can do that. But could I offer a suggestion first?"

Amelia sighed. "I thought you were going to work first."

"I've always been a strong advocate for the 'work smarter, not harder' approach to life. If organizing movies by year makes it easier for people to locate them, that's excellent. If, however, it's not the best organizational method, we'd save time and the business a good chunk of change by only organizing them once instead of organizing them once now and once later if you decide there's a better method."

Amelia clenched her jaw. "We've been here, in this location since 1978. And for nearly fifty years, we've been organized by release date. It's one of those things that keeps us who we are."

I let out a breath. "I don't want to overstep—"

"Then don't," Amelia said, cutting me off.

I nodded. "Okay."

Too soon.

While we were busy re-shelving tapes, I found myself unable to resist stealing glances at Amelia. With great enthusiasm, she animatedly conversed with a customer, her face brightening as she recommended a movie. It was clear she had a passion for this place, and I respected that. But passion alone wouldn't keep the doors open.

Jake joined me, grabbing a stack of tapes. "Thanks for doing this, man," he hissed. "Amelia has been under a lot of pressure. There's a communication gap between the town's desire to preserve its traditions and the store's attempts to appeal to the younger generations. We have to find a way to stay current while still respecting the essence of this place. Amelia's been through it, and this place means everything to her."

"I can see that," I said.

"When she found out the folks were going to sell, she tried to stay positive. When she found out that they couldn't find a buyer, she lost it."

"I only want to help."

Jake smiled, clapping me on the shoulder. "I know. I know that you're the one person I can count on. If anyone can turn this place around, it's you."

As we continued working, I couldn't help but notice how Amelia's eyes lingered on the old photographs and vintage trinkets, lost in the nostalgia of the store. I just hoped she wasn't clinging to the past, meticulously preserving every aspect, and that instead, she'd be ready to embrace change and let go. From what Jake had shared with me, the business model was no longer sustainable. In order to survive, they would have to make significant adjustments and adapt.

Then there was Jake's overprotectiveness. It was like Amelia was in a bubble that no one was allowed to penetrate. Before we even got to Rewind Rentals, Jake had pulled me aside.

"Look, man, I appreciate you coming out here to talk to Amelia. There's just one little thing." He'd straightened, cleared his throat, and narrowed his eyes. "I don't know what happened between you two in the past. But let's leave it there. Keep your dick out of my sister, and we're golden. Okay?"

I'd only nodded, surprised by his words. I'd assumed for all these years that Amelia had told her brother what happened between us. Either she hadn't, or this was Jake's way of putting his foot down.

"We good?" I asked.

"Yep."

We'd gone to Rewind after, and he hadn't brought it up again. I had a feeling he wouldn't, unless Amelia did. I sighed.

The day went on, and I slipped into a rhythm. Organizing the inventory, chatting with customers, and even handling the ancient cash register—all of it felt familiar. Now and then, I caught Amelia watching me, a mix of curiosity and skepticism in her eyes. With one glance, I realized she still held power over me.

She was still Amelia.

My best friend's sister.

By the time we closed the shop up for the night, we'd made significant progress. The store looked cleaner, more organized, and I could tell Amelia was pleased, even if she was trying to hide it.

"Thanks for your help today," she said, locking the doors. "I have to admit, you did a good job."

As I leaned against the doorframe, a warm smile played on my lips. "Glad to hear it. I meant what I said earlier—I'm here to help. Whatever you need."

She nodded, a small smile playing at the corners of her lips. "We'll see. Tomorrow, we tackle the inventory records."

"Looking forward to it," I said, watching her walk away. There was a determination in her step that I couldn't help admiring.

I headed to my car with Amelia on my mind. She was so passionate about film and preserving history. It was all she talked about today with her customers. In nearly every conversation I overheard, the customer asked about an obscure movie, and she had a story to go with every title. It wasn't just her extensive movie knowledge but also her ability to truly grasp and appreciate films that garnered admiration from everyone, including myself.

Her passion shone brightly, illuminating the world around her like a campfire on a summer night. It was contagious. The reason her organizational system worked so well was that Amelia knew every movie in that store. The reason it was a struggle for other folks was that they didn't want to ask. Not everyone would share her enthusiasm for talking about film.

At least, not yet. And if it meant spending more time with Amelia, well, that was a bonus I was more than willing to accept.

The next morning, I arrived at the store early, armed with two coffees and two cinnamon rolls from the local bakery, Knead the Dough.

"Good morning, Ams," I said, holding out a cup of coffee. "Thought you might need a pick-me-up."

She took the coffee, her expression softening. "Thanks. I could really use it today."

"Early morning or late night?"

Amelia's eyes narrowed. "I came back after grabbing some takeout and worked in the back room until two."

"You should have called me. I would have come over and helped," I said with a light chuckle.

Her eyebrows shot to the sky. "I just needed some time to clear my head."

I nodded, not really wanting to step on that minefield. "What's on the agenda for this morning?"

"I've pulled out the inventory records. It's a tedious task, but my parents never upgraded their digital inventory system," she said, passing a file to me. "The one we have works, but when you have to go through the store item by item, it can feel monotonous."

"I can have a list of inventory systems to you this afternoon, with links to play-test the software," I said, pivoting my strategy at her crinkled nose. "I love this old register so much. As a kid, I was in awe of how cool it looked to play with. These giant gold buttons here." I ran a finger over a few. "It's a privilege to finally get to press them."

"I don't know."

"We could pop this piece out here and run a power cord through that hole there," I said, walking her through my plan. "Then we put a tablet here, where the new display would have your point of sale, and on the customer's side, it would still be the old register."

Amelia's mouth twisted to the side, the gears in her brain ticking away. "Could you set it up in a way so that we could have multiple tablets that could access the same information for inventory?"

"Uh, yeah," I said, shocked she didn't shut me down. "I can definitely do that."

"Okay, email me the information, and I'll look at it tonight."

"I will do that."

"Thanks," Amelia said before grabbing a stack of papers and heading to the back room.

We spent the morning going through the inventory records, a tedious but necessary task. Understanding the scope of things was important. As we worked, we fell into a comfortable silence, interrupted only by the occasional question or comment. It was surprisingly easy, this partnership, and I found myself enjoying the work more than I expected.

By lunchtime, we'd made a significant dent in the records, and I suggested taking a break. "How about we grab some lunch?" I asked. "My treat."

Amelia hesitated before nodding. "Sure. Let's go to Golden Chopsticks. It's just over there," she said, pointing.

"I half expected you to say no," I said, only kind of joking.

"Why?" Amelia asked with a curious smile.

We walked together across the street. "I guess, given everything, I wasn't sure how comfortable you were with having me around."

She sighed. "I'm still not sure."

"I get that."

"But I know I'm glad you're here."

My heart skipped a beat. "Me too."

It felt good to be here, back home, with Amelia. We were seated right away and placed our orders after the server delivered our drinks.

"I know it sounds crazy," Amelia said, stirring her coffee. "But Rewind Rentals is more than just a store to me. It's part of my family's history. My grandparents started that place because of a deep love for film. My parents met there. I grew up there. I can't let it go. Not without a fight."

"It doesn't sound crazy at all," I said. "I get it. I want to help you keep Rewind. You know, I also grew up there. Maybe not in the same way, but it's part of my history. I can empathize with that."

Her eyes searched mine. "Why are you doing this, Flynn? You could be anywhere, doing anything. Why would you come back here when getting out of this town was the only thing you could talk about?"

I took a deep breath, choosing my words carefully. "Because I believe in this place. And I believe in you."

"That's not what I meant." Amelia crossed her arms.

"Because sometimes in life, you can be so sure you want certain things only to realize later you couldn't have been more wrong."

"Do you really think we can save her?"

"I wouldn't be here if I didn't."

Amelia cocked her head to the side. "Yes, you would. Don't lie."

I chuckled. "You're right; I would. But I'm not lying, Ams. I think that if we act as a team, we could save Rewind Rentals."

A genuine, warm grin spread across her face, illuminating her entire being. "Okay," she whispered. "Let's do it."

We finished eating and headed back to the store. I felt a sense of hope. It wasn't going to be easy saving this old place, but for the first time in a long time, I was excited about something.

THREE

Amelia

The unusual sense of optimism I felt this morning as I arrived at Rewind Rentals was unexpected. Flynn's presence was sudden, but his help was undeniably making a difference. My parents couldn't keep up anymore, and my teenage part-time help could only do so much. I looked forward to the day ahead, which was a strange feeling considering how overwhelming things had been lately.

I'd been coming and going from these front doors for nearly thirty years. From the creak of the door to the click of the light switch, everything about this place was familiar to me. It smelled like home. It was a comforting reminder of why I was fighting so hard to keep this place alive.

Growing up in this small town could feel limiting. There wasn't always a lot to do unless it was festival season. The nearest large shopping center was an hour away. Rewind Rentals was the highlight of so many youthful Friday nights.

I knew that things had changed and that, with the internet and streaming services, this shop was a dinosaur. I wasn't stupid; I knew what people said. The snide comments from the younger generations echoed in my heart with fear. I knew it was the right decision for Jake to ask for Flynn's help, especially considering Flynn's expertise in the matter.

The doorbell jingled, and the Devil walked in, carrying two coffees and a bag from Knead the Dough.

"Morning," Flynn said with a warm smile, passing me a coffee cup.

"Good morning, Flynn," I replied, accepting the coffee. "You don't have to keep doing this." I took a sip. "Mmm, thank you." I licked my lips.

He shrugged. "I figured if I'm getting myself one, I might as well get you one too. It'll help push us through another day of inventory records."

I chuckled and took another sip. "You might be right. Dorothea's has the most delicious treats."

Flynn passed me a bag, and I pulled out a slice of Inspiration Cake. It was lemon. "Oh, my favorite!"

We spent the morning diving into the inventory records. It was tedious work, but having Flynn there made it more bearable. He had a way of making even the most mundane tasks feel like they had a purpose.

"So, tell me," Flynn said, scanning through a stack of old rental forms. "What's your favorite movie?"

"That's a tough one. Here I thought you were going to ask why we've kept all these," I said, glancing up from my notebook. "But if I had to be honest and choose, I'd say *Before Sunrise* or *Before Sunset*. It's kind of a toss-up between the two."

"Really? I would have guessed you'd say *Casablanca* or something."

I laughed. "I mean, it's a classic and arguably a good choice. But I can't help it. The *Before* series is my favorite. It's like comfort food. It always feels good."

"Mine's *Clue*," Flynn said.

"Weird, I'd have pegged you for *The Godfather*." We both burst into a fit of laughter.

The conversation was natural, comfortable even. Two old friends falling back into an easy rhythm. We continued working, sharing our favorite movie moments and laughing over the ridiculous plots of some of the films in the inventory. It was easy, and for a moment, I forgot about the financial strain and the uncertainty of the future.

We'd made significant progress, and Flynn suggested we take a break. "How about another trip to Golden Chopsticks?" he asked, his eyes twinkling with mischief.

I smiled. "Sure, why not?"

We walked to the restaurant, and the conversation turned to our plans for the store. "I've been thinking," Flynn said as we took our seats. "We need to attract new customers. I have a few ideas for improvements that we can implement, but we should also think creatively."

"Okay, I'm listening," I said, unease settling into my belly. Change was never easy for me.

"So, we talked about the software update, and I sent you an email before we left the store."

"You did?"

Flynn smiled a toothy grin. "Sure did. I'm just that good."

"Thanks."

"I have some big ideas and some smaller ones. But all of them shape around the work we're doing now," he said. "The core problem with Rewind is that technology has evolved, and if we don't adapt, it will be left behind. For better or worse. We're not debating that point, right?"

I sighed. "No, we aren't." I wanted to, but I knew it was a pointless debate. Change was inevitable.

Under the table, Flynn's foot brushed against mine, the contact sending a spark of electricity through me. My breath caught in my throat. Was it an accident, or something more? I couldn't tell, but the thought of his foot resting so casually against mine made my pulse quicken.

Flynn leaned in, his voice low and intimate. "You've

grown even more beautiful, Amelia," he said, his eyes holding mine. It was hard to look away. "I missed seeing that smile."

I swallowed hard, my throat suddenly dry. I tried to muster a response, something casual, but all I could manage was a soft, "Thank you." My mind was too focused on the warmth of his foot against mine, and the way his gaze seemed to strip away every defense I had.

"What do you think about expanding your services?" Flynn asked, breaking my thoughts.

"Uh, what do you mean? We have a lot of movies that could go out, but there's only so much shelf space."

"Stay with me on this one. If we clean out the storage room behind the desk, remove the door, paint it bright sunshine yellow, line the walls with shelves, and turn it into an equipment inventory space for rentals. I know this might cost more than you anticipated as far as changes go, but I think there's really something here. If you expand to offer VHS players, record players, DVD and laserdisc players, and even retro video games, I think you could expand your offers to appeal to a much larger crowd."

"I'm listening."

"Most of the stores here in Coral Cove survive on the tourist industry. You need to tap into that deep well of growth," Flynn took a sip of his water.

"By renting out equipment?" I asked, more than a bit skeptical.

He nodded. "Yeah. There are lots of ways that we can really make this place a destination, and I have ideas for that too. We start with sprucing things up. Yes, we've been doing that. I'm thinking bigger."

"Like what?" I played with my napkin, hoping he wasn't about to go off the rails.

"I've been watching you."

This stopped me short. "Stalker much?"

Flynn chuckled. "You're so passionate about the films and their history, tidbits of knowledge about the way something was filmed, why, or how. You light up every time a customer comes in asking about a film." Flynn found my eyes and seemed to see into my soul. "I'm suggesting that we use your love of film to guide these changes."

The waiter brought by our lunch and refilled our drinks.

"Okay, I'm still listening," I said.

Flynn smiled. "I have connections in the independent film industry, and they are currently working on a documentary about outdated technology. I would like to reach out to them and inquire about the possibility of trading interviews and store access for their film, in exchange for doing some small filming and voice-over work for Rewind. I'd like to record you talking about the films you love. My goal is to enhance the engagement and historical aspect of Rewind Rentals."

"Could we shoot video, or would it be more like a song?" I asked.

"I'm considering capturing videos of collectibles, films, and even the filming sites of that movie that was made here in the early 2000s." Flynn shoved a bite of sweet and sour chicken into his mouth. "Mmm. I forgot how good this was."

"Okay."

"Okay?" he asked.

"Okay, call your friend and see if they're interested in using Rewind Rentals for their movie," I said.

"Alrighty then, I'll make the call today."

"What other ideas did you have?"

"What are your thoughts on hosting events, like a movie night or film trivia?"

I nodded, intrigued by the idea. "That could work. We used to have movie nights years ago, but we stopped them because attendance dropped off. We have a giant room upstairs, and my grandparents set up an old projector. I always thought it would be great to bring in a bunch of couches and chairs. Really comfy stuff and serve popcorn, candy, you know? Maybe it's time to bring them back?"

"Exactly," Flynn said, leaning forward. "We can market it on social media, get the word out. Create some buzz. Bring in a popcorn machine and candy. I think it would have a lot of potential. I have a furniture guy as well."

"Of course you do," I laughed and took a bite of my rice. I hesitated, the familiar doubt creeping in. "But what if it doesn't work? What if we put in all this effort and still don't make enough to keep the store open?"

Flynn reached across the table, his hand covering mine. "We won't know unless we try, Amelia."

His touch was warm, reassuring, and I believed him. For better or worse, what was a few thousand dollars and a failed try? The store would close if we didn't do something.

"Okay," I breathed. "Let's do it."

After lunch, we headed back to the store with a renewed sense of purpose. Flynn set up a makeshift office in the back of the room, and we started brainstorming ideas for movie nights. We created a list of potential themes, from classic film noir to 80s nostalgia, and began drafting a marketing plan.

As the afternoon wore on, the store filled with customers, and I found myself feeling more and more excited. Organizing the inventory, chatting with regulars, and even handling the ancient cash register—it all felt familiar.

Flynn was right there beside me, effortlessly chatting with customers and making them feel welcome. His presence brought a new energy to the store, one I hadn't realized was missing until now. Maybe it was his casual demeanor, the way he treated every stranger off the street like they were an old friend. It was disarming, and I could see how people were drawn to him.

By closing time, we were both exhausted but filled with a renewed exhilaration, the kind that comes from a day well spent.

"Thanks for today," I said, turning the key in the lock. When I glanced up, Flynn was leaning against the doorway, looking far more attractive than he had any right to. The musky, woodsy scent of him filled the air between us, intoxicating and impossible to ignore.

"Glad to hear it. I meant what I said earlier—I'm here to help. Whatever it takes," Flynn said, nodding, a small smile tugging at the corners of his lips.

"I'll see you tomorrow," I replied, waving goodbye.

"Looking forward to it," he added, his voice low and smooth, almost a purr.

I watched him walk away, his confident stride making it hard to look away. As much as I was starting to recognize the value he brought, a nagging voice in the back of my mind reminded me that letting him in was a risk. He left me once before, and the fear that he could do it again lingered. I needed to stay focused on saving the store, not on someone who might bail on me when I needed them most.

FOUR

Flynn

Cleaning out the back room proved to be more of a workout than I'd anticipated. Dust swirled in the air, catching the light streaming through the small window, and my muscles ached from moving boxes and old equipment. Amelia was just as dedicated, sorting through piles of old VHS tapes, DVDs, and even film canisters. She moved with an intensity that only she could muster.

"Hey, Amelia," I called out, pulling a large, dusty projector from a corner. "Look at this. I didn't know your grandparents had one of these."

Amelia glanced up, her eyes widening. "Wow, that's ancient. I think they used it for movie nights way back in the day."

"We should clean it up and see if it still works," I suggested, already feeling a surge of excitement at the idea.

"Good idea," she said, smiling. "It could be a great addition to our movie nights."

"Do you have any reels for it?"

"Yeah, those film canisters over there," she pointed to a shelf stacked with giant round metal containers.

"Wicked."

We spent the next hour cleaning and setting up the projector, our hands brushing occasionally as we worked side by side. Each touch sent a jolt through me. I shook it away, reminding myself why I was here. Amelia needed help saving the store, not a complicated romantic entanglement.

"Okay, moment of truth," I said as I loaded an old film reel labeled 'Opening Day' onto the projector. "Let's see if this thing still works."

The projector whirred to life, casting a flickering image on the wall. We watched in amazement as the scenes from the store's opening day played out before us. The footage was grainy, but it was charming, showing Amelia's grandparents welcoming their first customer.

"This is incredible," Amelia whispered, her eyes glistening with nostalgia.

As the film continued to play, I couldn't help but feel a deep connection to this place. It wasn't just about saving a store. It was about preserving a piece of history, a legacy that meant so much to Amelia and her family. I glanced at her, noticing the soft smile on her lips as she watched the old footage. Her passion for Rewind Rentals was palpable, and I admired her more for it.

"Flynn, look at this," she said, her voice filled with excitement. She pointed to a scene in the film where her grandparents were standing. "They used to host all kinds of educational movies with the local kids and the library. They were really into giving back to the community."

"That's amazing," I said. "We could bring something like that back. Make it part of our community outreach."

Amelia nodded, her eyes shining. "Yeah, I think that would be wonderful. It's a way to honor their legacy and also bring more people in."

As we watched the footage, a peculiar energy seemed to vibrate through the room, making the hairs on my arms stand on end. Suddenly, a bright flash of light erupted from the projector, illuminating the room with a brilliance that seemed to pause time for a moment. Amelia and I both jumped back, shielding our eyes.

When the light faded, we turned to look at the wall. The film continued to play. But something wasn't right. Hanging on the dusty wall was a faded movie poster, one neither of us remembered seeing before.

"What the heck is that?" Amelia asked.

I stepped closer, examining the poster. "It's that old classic by Hitchcock, *The Birds*." I couldn't shake the feeling that it hadn't been there before.

"Was that always there?" I asked, glancing at Amelia, who shook her head slowly.

"I'm not sure. How odd..." she murmured, touching the edge of the poster gingerly.

We didn't make a big deal of it, chalking it up to a trick of the light or an overlooked relic from the past. But as we returned to our work, the poster remained, its presence a silent testament to the magic that lingered in the air of Rewind Rentals.

We spent the next hour lost in the memories captured on the film. It was a beautiful reminder of what Rewind Rentals stood for and why it was worth fighting for. When the reel ended, we sat in silence for a moment, letting the nostalgia wash over us.

"I'm glad you're here, Flynn," Amelia said. A smile played at her lips. "I don't think I could do this without you."

Her words took me by surprise, and I felt a warmth spread through my chest. "I'm glad to be here too, Amelia."

As we continued working over the next week, I started implementing some of my ideas. I brought in a team to update the store's electronic filing system. At first, Amelia resisted, clinging to the old ways, but as my guy highlighted the advantages, her perspective shifted. It made managing the inventory easier and allowed us to focus more on the customer experience.

The more time we spent together, the more our shared history and unresolved feelings surfaced. One evening, as we were wrapping up for the night, Amelia turned to me, her expression serious. "Flynn, I need to ask you something."

"Sure, what is it?" I asked, a knot suddenly forming in my stomach.

"Why did you come back?" Her voice was barely above a whisper. "I mean, really come back. Was it just because Jake begged you for the sake of the store? Or was it something else?"

I took a deep breath, choosing my words carefully. "It started with the store, Amelia. But being here, working with you, it's made me realize that being here has always meant more. I missed Coral Cove, but more than that… I missed you."

She looked at me, her eyes searching mine for the truth. "I missed you too, Flynn," she admitted. "But I don't know if I can go back. A lot has changed in six years."

"You were counting?" I asked.

She shrugged.

"I'm not going anywhere, Amelia."

There was a moment before she replied. In that moment, it felt as though a weight had been lifted, and a sense of lightness washed over me. We stood there, surrounded by the history we were fighting to preserve. She reached for my hand. "I've heard that one before."

"Ouch. I guess I deserved that."

Amelia laced her fingers in mine. Maybe all wasn't lost.

FIVE

Amelia

A s I drifted off to sleep, a feeling of hope washed over me, something I hadn't experienced in quite some time. The following morning, I arrived at the store with a sense of purpose. Today was the day we would begin its beautification transformation, and this old storage space was getting a remodel.

"Morning, Ams," Flynn called out, pushing the door open with his shoulder as he balanced two coffees and a bag of pastries from Knead the Dough.

"Morning," I replied, looking up from the counter where I was cleaning up some paperwork I'd left out the night before. My eyes brightened when I saw the coffee. "You're spoiling me at this point. I hope you understand you'll never be able to stop bringing the coffee. You will forever be required to bring treats after I appoint you the King of the Bakery. It's a rule. I didn't make it. I'm just the enforcer."

From a deep guttural place, Flynn chuckled. "Just trying to keep us both motivated," he said, handing me a cup. "Today's going to be busy."

The first part of the morning was spent finalizing our plans for the back room. Just like he promised, Flynn had called a buddy making a film about technology, and they were super excited to come out and see the shop. They were eager to start filming.

Flynn and I worked side by side, clearing out the last of the old equipment and setting up the new shelving units. The back room was slowly transforming into a bright, inviting space. Per his suggestion, we painted the walls a cheerful sunflower yellow. We didn't have all the new products in the mail yet, but true to his word, Flynn had connections. We got a good deal on vintage systems.

Around noon, Flynn's friend Rory arrived with her film crew. She was a tall, dark-haired, strikingly beautiful woman with an air of confidence about her. Rory's approach sent a wave of unease through me.

"Flynn, it's so good to see you," Rory said, pulling him into a quick hug. "I've been looking forward to this since you mentioned it weeks ago."

Weeks ago? It's only been... I tried to do the math, but everything felt like a blur. Had Flynn been planning from day one? Maybe before he was back in town?

"Same. I really appreciate you doing me a solid." Flynn returned her hug. "This is Amelia, the heart and soul of Rewind Rentals."

Rory turned to me with a warm smile. "It's truly a pleasure to meet you, Amelia. Flynn's told me so much about you and this amazing little store."

"Nice to meet you too," I said.

There, I was polite. I didn't shoot her daggers or make a snide comment.

Rory didn't seem to notice my hesitation. She immediately started discussing the plans for the video, gesturing animatedly and outlining her vision for us.

As Flynn and Rory talked, I couldn't help but feel a bubble of jealousy grow inside me.

I had zero reason to be jealous. We weren't officially

anything. Flynn said he wasn't going anywhere. And that sounded great, but it was overshadowed by the past. He left once before, and just because he said he wasn't going anywhere didn't mean he was staying for me.

Love for Flynn had consumed me for years. Ever since a barbecue at the neighbor's house in the sixth grade. Back when my mom and his mom were friends, before his parents split. Before he and Jake became inseparable. Flynn Callahan was my world.

And then he left, and my world shattered.

We spent the next few hours filming different segments of the store. I felt awkward at first, but Flynn's encouragement helped, and I found my rhythm. Rory was professional and efficient, directing her crew with ease.

During a break, I went outside looking for some air. Flynn found me a couple of minutes later.

"You okay?" he asked.

"Yeah, I'm fine," I said, but my voice lacked conviction. "Rory seems really...friendly." That was as much kindness as I could muster. The green monster inside of me was rearing her ugly head.

Flynn glanced through the window at Rory, who was chatting with one of her crew members. "Rory? She's just enthusiastic. We've known each other our whole lives."

My eyes narrowed. "How well do you know her?"

Flynn seemed to understand what was bothering me. "Amelia, Rory is my cousin. She lived in another state, so we didn't see much of each other until six years ago." He rubbed the back of his head uncomfortably. "That's when she moved to the area for school. She stayed with me for a while. She loved it so much, she stuck around. There's nothing between us but family."

Relief flooded through me. "I didn't know. I thought..." I trailed off, too embarrassed to finish the thought.

"I get it," Flynn said gently. "But you don't have to worry about her or anyone else."

Everything in me wanted to believe him.

We stood close, so close that I could feel the warmth radiating from his body. The air between us crackled with tension, every breath I took filled with his scent, his presence. Flynn's hand reached up slowly, his fingers brushing against my cheek as he tucked a strand of hair behind my ear. The touch was gentle, almost hesitant, but it sent a shockwave through me, making my heart pound.

"I've spent years regretting my choices. Whatever this is, I'm not going to mess it up. Not again." He leaned in ninety percent of the way. His eyes full of heat.

Our eyes met, and for a moment, time seemed to stand still. I could see the conflict in Flynn's eyes, the same war raging within me. I wanted to step back, to put some distance between us, but my body betrayed me, leaning into his touch instead. I was drawn to him, like a moth to a flame, and I knew I was about to get burned.

When Flynn finally closed the distance and kissed me, it was slow, deliberate, as if he were savoring every second. His lips were soft, warm, and the kiss was filled with years of unspoken words, pent-up desires. I melted into him, my hands finding their way to his chest, clutching at the fabric of his shirt as if he were the only thing keeping me grounded. The kiss deepened, becoming more urgent, more needy, until we were both breathless, the world around us forgotten.

I thought about all the things that had passed between us. All the firsts we shared. All of my most important firsts were with Flynn. Did I want my others to be with him, too?

I inhaled him. Longing and passion intertwined as our tongues danced in harmony. Flynn ran a hand through my hair, pulling me closer.

Someone cleared their throat loudly.

We pulled apart to find Rory standing there. "I don't mean to interrupt but—"

"Oh my stars, I'm so sorry. Yes, let's, um," I brushed my shirt and hair down.

Flynn was as composed as ever, completely unbothered by the fact that we were caught in the act.

"I'm so sorry," I said again.

Rory laughed. "No worries at all. Really, it's totally fine."

We went inside and continued working. The atmosphere in the room lightened considerably. Rory's crew captured some fantastic footage of the memorabilia we had in the original spaces upstairs and down.

Rory approached me with a request. "Amelia, would you mind sitting down for an interview? I really think your story and passion for the store would add a lot to the documentary."

I hesitated for a moment, but Flynn's reassuring nod gave me the confidence I needed. "Sure, I'd be happy to."

Rory set up a chair in front of the camera and adjusted the lighting. "Just relax and speak from your heart," she said with a smile. "We want to capture your genuine love for this place."

I took a deep breath and sat down, feeling a mix of nervous excitement.

Rory started with a soft, encouraging tone. "Amelia, can you tell us about your earliest memory of Rewind Rentals?"

I smiled, letting the nostalgia wash over me. "It's the buttery smell of popcorn and watching *The Little Princess* on the old projector. I must have been around five years old. My grandparents ran the store back then. Every Friday night, my grandma and I would cuddle up on one of the couches. It was my favorite weekly ritual. This place has always felt like home."

Rory nodded, her eyes bright with interest. "What

inspired you to take over the store and keep it running after all these years?"

"My parents wanted to sell the store and retire," I said, my voice growing more passionate. "But I couldn't let that happen. This store is more than just a business to me. It's a piece of our family's history and a vital part of the community. People come here not just to rent movies, but to relive memories, to connect with something tangible in a world that's gone digital."

Rory leaned forward slightly, encouraging me to continue. "How has Flynn's return impacted the store?"

I glanced at Flynn, who was watching from behind the camera with an encouraging smile. "Flynn's return has been a game-changer. He brought fresh ideas and a new energy that we desperately needed. He's helped us modernize without losing the charm that makes Rewind Rentals special. And more than that, he reminded me why this place is worth fighting for."

Rory's next question was more personal. "What has been the most challenging part of this journey for you?"

I took a moment to gather my thoughts. "The uncertainty has been the hardest part. Not knowing if we'd make it, if all the hard work would pay off. But every time I see a customer's face light up when they find a movie they loved as a kid, it reminds me we're doing something important."

Rory smiled warmly. "What do you hope for the future of Rewind Rentals?"

"I hope it continues to be a place where people can come to reconnect with the past and create new memories," I said. "I want it to be a community hub, a place that brings people together. And with all the changes we're making, I believe that can happen."

By the end of the day, we had a lot of material to work with. The back room looked incredible, and the store was coming together.

Rory approached me with a smile. "You were amazing, Amelia. Your passion for this place is truly inspiring."

"Thank you," I said, genuinely touched. "I'm glad we're doing this. It's going to help so much."

"That's the plan," Rory said with a wink. "We'll edit this footage and get it back to you in a couple of weeks. Flynn said he mentioned my movie to you and that we might be able to use the footage for our film?"

"Yes! Oh yes, please use whatever you like."

"You are a passionate woman who is all about saving the last video rental store on the west coast," Rory said with such enthusiasm. "You know these films in and out. More than that, you're passionate about film. I've been watching you today."

My cheeks grew warm. "I'm flattered you see me that way."

After Rory and her crew left, Flynn and I stood in the newly transformed back room, looking around with pride.

"This is incredible, Flynn," I said, my voice filled with awe. "Thank you for all your help."

"None of this would have been possible if it wasn't for you. This is all you, Ams. And it's not over yet." Flynn grinned. "We still have a lot of work to do. But we're getting there."

I nodded, my eyes meeting his. "Yeah, we sure are."

SIX

Flynn

The transformation of Rewind Rentals was well underway, and our first movie night was finally here. We had spread the word through social media and flyers around town, hoping for a good turnout. I arrived at the store early to help Amelia set up.

Amelia and I hadn't talked about the kiss we shared the other day. The right time would come around, and I wasn't going to push it.

"Morning, Flynn," Amelia greeted me with a smile as she arranged stacks of candy on the counter.

"Morning, Ams. How are we feeling about tonight?" I asked, grabbing a stack of vintage movie posters that still needed frames before being hung.

"Nervous, but I think mostly I'm excited," she admitted. "I really hope this works."

"It will work," I said confidently. "We've put in a lot of hard work. People are going to love it."

As the day went on, we finished setting up the store, transforming it into a cozy, nostalgic haven. The bright yellow walls of the back room now showcased vintage VHS, DVD, and record players. There were old movie posters on the

33

walls. We had expanded our inventory as well. It was all a work in progress, but there had been huge strides.

Upstairs, we set up the old projector and arranged two dozen couches and a half circle of bean bags in the front to create a cozy theater viewing area. There were stacks of blankets, lots of extra pillows, and I even installed drink holders on the sides of each couch. The room could comfortably hold one hundred audience members, and the fire chief said we could have one hundred twenty people in that space.

Before the customers headed upstairs, they could buy any number of different candies, sodas, and, of course, fresh hot buttery popcorn. We programmed an intermission halfway through the films so that customers could stretch, come downstairs, and replenish their snacks.

Every aspect of expanding the business with the single theater lounge and the system rentals was a strategic move to increase sales. Hypothetically, with five showings a week, Rewind Rentals' profits would increase at such a substantial rate, it would allow Amelia to stay open and for her parents to retire. If there was more than one showing a day, it could be more. She was struggling to believe it still, but tonight I hoped to give her a glimpse of the future I planned.

By the time evening rolled around, a crowd had gathered. Locals and tourists alike filled the store, their faces lighting up with excitement as they took in the new retro ambiance.

"Welcome to the first movie night at Rewind Rentals!" Amelia announced, her voice carrying a mix of nervousness and enthusiasm. "Tonight, we're showing *The Goonies*, a classic adventure film that we hope you'll all enjoy. If you haven't had a chance to purchase some of our fresh popcorn or grab an icy cold drink, you still have time before the movie starts. After you've got your tickets, head upstairs to find a comfy spot."

As the movie started, I watched the crowd settle in, their eyes glued to the screen. There was a palpable sense of community in the air, a shared appreciation for the nostalgia and magic of old movies.

About halfway through the movie, right before we called intermission, something strange happened. During the scene where the kids find the treasure map, suddenly the room went bright white before going back to the film. No one was bothered, thank the stars above. We'd have to look at the film and projector. I thought I'd fixed the issue from the last time. But I guess not. I wondered if maybe it was missing a cell? I'd have to call someone to be sure.

Amelia and I went downstairs to run the concessions. It was the oddest thing. Behind the counter, hanging on the wall, was an old map that looked an awful lot like the one in the movie upstairs. I blinked, not quite believing what I was seeing.

"Amelia, when did you buy that?" I whispered, nudging her.

She turned, and her eyes widened. "I assumed that was you."

"It was not. I have no idea where it came from," I said, taking it off the wall. "I don't remember it being here earlier."

"That's because it wasn't," Amelia said. "Jake?" she called out.

Jake popped his head out from behind a shelf. He was working this evening. "What's up?"

"When did you hang this map?" I asked.

"I didn't," he said. "These changes are all you."

We exchanged puzzled looks, but just then a group of folks trotted down the stairs for more concessions, gossiping about how much they loved the new space. Customers quickly surrounded us, inundating us with questions.

By the time the intermission was over, I'd forgotten about the map. The rest of the movie played, and when the film ended, Amelia and I stood up to address the crowd.

"Thank you all for coming tonight!" Amelia said, beaming. The crowd erupted with applause. "We hope you enjoyed the movie. We're planning to host themed movie nights and film trivia nights, and private events, so please spread the word. The calendar is up downstairs, and you can grab a flyer of events on your way out. We want Rewind Rentals to be a place where the community can come together and share their love for movies."

As people filed out, a few of them approached. "So, we were just having a debate, and we were hoping you could clear something up for us. You know the map hanging behind the register? That wasn't there earlier, was it?"

Amelia and I locked eyes.

"Well, you see that old projector up there?" I said, really leaning into the question. "I'm not saying it was the projector, but I'm also not not saying it was the projector."

They all chuckled at my joke. But the reality was, we had no idea. We weren't the only ones to notice its arrival. We were excited about the gift all the same.

Once everyone left, the store was quiet, the excitement of the night still lingering in the air. Jake went home after complaining that he had to be up early for work. This left Amelia and me alone to clean up the remnants of popcorn and empty cups.

"That was an unequivocal success," I said, smiling at her. "People really seemed to enjoy themselves."

"They did," she agreed, her eyes shining with happiness. "And that map... I don't know how it got here, but it definitely added to the mystique of this place."

"Right? It was the cherry on top of a nearly perfect evening," I said.

We stood there for a moment, the energy between us crackling with unspoken words.

"What would have made it better?" Amelia asked, her voice growing husky.

Before I could think twice, I reached out and pulled her

close, our lips meeting in a fiery kiss. All the tension and longing from the past six years exploded between us in that moment.

The time we'd lost melted away. A rush of memories and firsts. Amelia was my entire world and every one of my favorite memories.

With her hands tangled in my hair, she pulled me closer, silently begging for more. My hand gently wrapped around her waist, exploring the softness beneath her shirt and reveling in the intimate warmth between our bodies. Outside the store, the bustling sounds of the town faded into a distant murmur, creating a tranquil bubble for just the two of us.

The past collided with the present as if nothing could come between us again. I unhooked her bra and slipped her shirt off, exposing her supple breasts. Amelia had my top off in an equal frenzy.

"Flynn," she said, her voice breathless as she urgently tugged on my belt loop, leading me to a soft beanbag. With a sudden force, she tugged me on top of her, our bodies pressed together.

"Amelia, I…" I trailed off, unable to finish the thought, too enamored by the scent of her and the way her nails dug into my back, pulling me closer.

"Shhh," she whispered. "Make love to me?"

"Your wish is my command," I murmured, my kisses tracing a delicate line from her neck down to the gentle curve of her breast. I took a nipple into my mouth, savoring its sweetness, while my free hand explored all of her soft curves.

Amelia's moan of pleasure echoed through the room, a testament to the sheer bliss she was experiencing. "More," she demanded.

I took my time, sliding her pants off with care, relishing the sight that unfolded before my eyes. She was round in all the right places, with the most luscious, bitable thighs.

She squirmed under my gaze. "Flynn?"

"I'm drinking you in, baby," I said before finding her lips again. With each passing second, our kiss became more passionate, igniting a primal urge within me that I struggled to contain.

Instead, I explored her body with my lips, planting kisses and teasing bites along the way until I discovered the intense warmth and moisture at her core. I gently spread her legs further apart, then I wrapped them over my shoulders and pulled her wet pussy closer. Her slick heat tantalized my taste buds, and I relished savoring every last drop.

"Oh god," Amelia panted.

I lapped at her pussy, slowly making my way to her clit. I flicked it with my tongue, writing a love poem, willing it to find her heart.

I sucked gently, feeling her body tense beneath me. Her breath came in shallow gasps, and her hands gripped my hair, urging me on. Her moans grew louder, echoing off the walls as she reached the peak of pleasure.

I let the pleasure climb before laying her back down, stripping the last of my clothes. My aching cock found her center, poised to join us together.

Before I entered her, I met Amelia's eyes. She nodded, her gaze filled with trust and longing, and in one smooth action, I was inside her. Her heat enveloped me, and it almost sent me over the edge.

"Please," Amelia begged, her voice a sultry whisper.

I thrust again, and again. Faster and faster, our bodies moving in perfect harmony. She clung to me, her nails making art on my back, and I felt the sweet, intoxicating pull of pleasure building within me.

As I shifted, I lifted one of her legs for better access to her clit, entering her again with renewed urgency. That was all it took; Amelia cried out in pleasure, her release washing over her in waves. I reveled in her ecstasy, feeling her body quiver around me. For a brief moment, I wondered if she'd stir the attention of the neighbors. It was a fleeting thought, gone quicker than it came. I pumped inside her again and found my own release, the world fading away until there was only us.

When we finally broke apart, we were breathless, our eyes locked on one another. Her skin glowed, and her smile was radiant, as if she had been waiting for this moment as long as I had.

"Flynn," she whispered, her voice trembling with either emotion or the aftershocks of orgasm. Which, I couldn't tell.

In the dim light of the store, I confessed, "I've missed you so much, Amelia." I brushed a strand of hair from her face, my heart swelling with emotion. "This feels right," I mumbled. "Being here with you, working in this place... it all feels like it was meant to be."

She shifted slightly, her expression growing serious. Her smile faltered for just a moment as if she was wrestling with an unspoken thought. "Why did you leave me then?"

I blinked, surprised by her question. "I'm here right now," I said, not sure where this was coming from. I thought we'd moved past it. Left the past in the past.

Her eyes shifted, downcast. "Why did you leave six years ago?"

I hesitated, the weight of her question settling heavily in the space between us. "I…" I began, my voice faltering. I took a deep breath, realizing that now, more than ever, she deserved the truth.

SEVEN

Amelia

Our first movie night was a wild success. Customers poured out in support of the lovingly named The Rewind Theatre. We had to turn people away when we met capacity.

Jake explained that those who couldn't catch the film rented movies. He'd even rented out half of our stock of VHS players and had reservations come in for future dates. In every possible way, this marked the greatest accomplishment the store had ever experienced.

It was an undeniable success.

Yet, as I lay here in the dim light, tangled in Flynn's arms, the question I'd buried for so long rose to the surface, insistent and relentless.

"Why did you leave six years ago?" I asked, my voice barely above a whisper. The words hung heavy in the air between us, casting a shadow over the warmth we'd just shared.

"I…" Flynn's eyes searched mine, and I could see the conflict warring inside him. "Amelia, it wasn't about you. It was never about you."

"How could it not be?" I wondered. "Then what was it?" I

pressed, my heart aching with the memories of his sudden departure.

He sighed, running a hand through his tousled hair. "I got an offer I couldn't refuse—a job that promised everything I thought I wanted. I was young, Amelia. Ambitious and scared of being tied down before I had the chance to find out who I was."

My chest cracked open at his words. I pushed back, needing more space between us. "So, you just left?" I asked, the bitterness creeping into my voice despite my efforts to suppress it.

"I know it sounds selfish," Flynn admitted. "I needed to prove to myself that I could make it on my own. I got so caught up that I completely lost sight of what mattered."

"And what about us?" I asked, feeling the old wound reopening. "Did I mean anything to you?"

"How can you ask that? Of course you did," Flynn said, his eyes earnest. "You meant everything, but back then, I wasn't ready for everything. I thought I needed to be someone else. I thought I had to find my own success, and instead, I found I was wrong. I'd given up the most important thing in my life to chase a dream that left me unfulfilled."

"You didn't even call." I reached for a blanket, wrapping it around myself.

"Because I knew if you asked me to stay, I would have stayed. There was no way I could have looked into your October eyes and said no. I would have given up everything for you. I would have bent the world in two just to see you smile. I stayed away because I couldn't be who you wanted me to be."

"I only ever wanted you," I said, tears falling down my cheeks. "You didn't have to be something different for me."

"I know," Flynn said, his voice a whisper.

"And what's changed? How do I know you won't just

pick up and leave again when something better comes along?"

Flynn reached for my hand, but I pulled away, needing space between us to breathe and think. "I've changed, Amelia. I've seen what life is like without you, without Coral Cove, without family. It's not where I want to be. I'm here now because this is where I belong."

I couldn't meet his eyes.

"I spent the last six years trying to be the kind of man you could come home to. You are everything. You always have been. Since that first time we met as kids."

"You were Jake's friend," I said, a bit harsher than I intended.

"Because I was too afraid to ask to be yours."

Silence settled between us, thick with unspoken doubts and lingering hurt. I wanted to believe him—I really did. But part of me was still that young girl who watched him walk away without a backward glance.

The weight of our past pressed down on me, threatening to drown out the happiness we'd found again. I took a deep breath, trying to calm the storm brewing inside me. "I want to believe you, Flynn, but I don't know how."

He nodded, understanding in his eyes. "I know, and I don't blame you. But I'm going to prove it to you, every day. I'm not going anywhere, Amelia. I'm in this for the long haul."

I nodded, my heart torn between hope and fear. "I guess we'll see."

Flynn gave me a small reassuring smile, but the tension between us lingered, a reminder of the unresolved issues we still had to face.

The success of The Rewind Theater brought in a wave of new customers, and with it, new challenges. The store was busier than ever, and we juggled the increased demand with the logistical issues of running a growing business. Flynn and

I worked tirelessly, side by side, for four days, but the strain of our unresolved conversations simmered beneath the surface.

Things weren't right between us yet. I don't know if they ever would be. The sudden rush of customers provided a welcome distraction, allowing me a few precious moments of reprieve.

The town buzzed with excitement over the magic at Rewind Rentals. Word spread quickly about the mysterious map, and soon enough, people were flocking to the store, hoping to witness some magic for themselves.

The next night, when we showed the film *Rear Window*, a pair of binoculars appeared on a shelf in the theater with over seventy witnesses. Everyone wanted to know the secret to the magic. We didn't have any more answers now than the first time it had happened. It was great for business.

Flynn was busy fixing the old sound system. We weren't quite ready for that upgrade just yet, when a man in a sleek suit walked into the store. He introduced himself as David Reed, a representative from a "larger entertainment company"—as if he couldn't just tell us who he was really with. He was interested in purchasing Rewind Rentals and The Rewind Theater in key ready.

"You are all the buzz," David said, flashing a polished smile. "We believe this place has incredible potential. I came here today to make you an offer, Ms. Bennet."

I was taken aback. "Buy the store? But why?" Not that I hadn't thought about it. Before deciding to try and save it myself, I carefully considered and explored every available option.

David leaned forward, his expression serious. "We think Rewind Rentals could be the centerpiece of a new chain of retro movie experiences. With your unique touch and our resources, it could be something spectacular."

My mind raced. On one hand, I'd be lying if I didn't say

the offer was tempting. It promised financial security and the chance to expand on a scale I hadn't dared to dream of. But on the other hand, the store was my family's legacy. Could I really sell it?

Flynn joined us, his expression guarded. "What kind of offer are we talking about?"

Flynn's eyes widened as I showed him the folder with a neatly typed proposal. The amount they were willing to pay was staggering. I glanced at him, seeing the same conflict mirrored in his eyes.

"I can see that you'll need some time to think on it," David said, smoothing his suit. "Take all the time you need."

I couldn't find the words to reply.

"Thank you," Flynn said, his tone firm.

"I'll be in touch," David said before leaving the store.

As Flynn and I stood there, the weight of the choice bore down on me, filling the silence. It was my family legacy, and ultimately, my decision.

"What do you think?" I finally asked, breaking the tension.

Flynn rubbed the back of his neck, deep in thought. "I think his timing is weird. Like, where did he come from? Why would he want to buy something in this little town? But on the other hand, it's a lot of money, Amelia. More than you'd ever likely see otherwise. But is it worth giving up what you've built here?"

"I don't know," I admitted, my heart heavy with indecision. "This place means so much to me, to my family. I don't want to lose that."

"You should probably sleep on it. Weigh your options. We've worked hard to make this place what it is. You don't have to decide now if you want to keep fighting for it."

As I nodded, a strong sense of resolve settled deep within me. "This place has always been more than just a business to me. It's my home."

Flynn smiled, reaching out to take my hand. "I'll support whatever decision you make. If you want to sell, I know a lawyer in town that could offer some advice. If you want to fight to keep it, I'll fight with you."

I let him hold my hand. The warmth of him was reassuring. It seemed I had two choices to make now.

EIGHT

T he day after meeting David Reed, the air felt thicker, filled with the weight of his proposal and the uncertainty it brought with it. Rewind Rentals had always been a haven, a constant in my previously chaotic life. Now, it felt like it was on the precipice of change, teetering between the familiar past and an uncertain future.

Amelia's parents had called her earlier that morning, announcing their official retirement. I knew this was something she had been anticipating for a while, but the timing couldn't have been worse. It was as if everything was happening at once, converging into a singular point of stress and decision.

"Amelia, your parents called again," I said, putting down the phone after they'd asked to speak with her. "How are you feeling about everything?"

She sighed, running a hand through her hair. "It's a lot to take in. I mean, I always knew they'd retire someday, but now it's real. They want to travel, spend time with friends. It's like they're finally letting go, and I have to be ready to carry this legacy on my own."

"You're not alone, Amelia. I'm here," I reassured her.

"I know. It's just a lot," she said, her voice laced with a mix of excitement and apprehension. "I just need to make sure we don't lose everything they've worked so hard for."

"We won't," I said firmly, trying to instill confidence in her and myself. "Whatever happens, whatever you decide, it will be okay," I said, as if saying it out loud would make it true.

Amelia nodded, taking the phone. "Hey, Mom."

With the store bustling and new customers flocking in to see the "magical" Rewind Rentals, I found myself increasingly fascinated by the mysterious events that were unfolding. The old map, the binoculars, and now we had a baseball bat from *Pride of the Yankees* and a yearbook from *The Graduate* with actual pictures from the high school in the film…they couldn't all be coincidences. There had to be something more, something tied to the very essence of this place.

Driven by curiosity and the need to understand, I dug deeper into the store's origins. Maybe there was a logical explanation as to why Rewind Rentals always seemed to be at the epicenter. I wanted to know why Amelia's grandparents had stopped showing films if they knew about the magic and what it could mean for us now.

I made my way to Spellbound Stories, the local bookstore known for its eclectic collection of rare books on local lore. The inside of the cozy little shop was designed to look like you've just walked into a fantasy novel. There were towering shelves and the comforting smell of new and aged paper. As I entered, I was greeted by a dark-haired man with an easy smile.

"Welcome, I'm Park. Let me know if there's anything specific you're looking for," he said, his voice warm and inviting.

"I'm Flynn," I replied, shaking his hand. "I'm actually looking for information about the history of Rewind Rentals.

It's had some...interesting things happen recently, and I'm trying to figure out why."

Park raised an eyebrow, intrigued. "Rewind Rentals, huh? That place has quite a reputation. I think I might have something that could help."

He led me through the maze of bookshelves to a section dedicated to local history and legends. He pulled out a non-fiction book with a worn cover titled, *Mystical Happenings in Coral Cove*, and flipped through the pages until he found what he was looking for.

"Here you go," Park said, passing the book to me. "In a chapter about unusual spots in Coral Cove, Rewind is specifically mentioned. It turns out that even before it was a rental store, the place was known for its frequent occurrence of unexplained phenomena."

I scanned the page, taking in the stories of mysterious apparitions and objects appearing out of thin air. It was fascinating and unnerving at the same time. "This is incredible," I said, looking up at Park. "Do you know why these things happened there?"

Park nodded. "The book hints that the magic could be influenced by the original owner's deep connection to Coral Cove. The rumors were that they dabbled in the supernatural." Park shrugged. "But if you want to know more, you should talk to Lillian at the flower shop. She's been around a lot longer than most people realize, and she might have some insights that you won't find in any book."

"Can I buy this?" I asked, holding up the book.

"Sure thing," he said.

I thanked Park for his help and promised to return with an update if I learned anything. I left the store and couldn't shake the feeling that I was on the brink of discovering something monumental.

The Sunflower was a small, charming flower shop filled

with vibrant blooms and the soothing scent of lavender in the air. Lillian, the owner, was tending to a display of sunflowers when I walked in. She was an elegant woman with a timeless aura about her. Her eyes twinkled with the wisdom of someone who had seen much in her lifetime.

"Flynn Callahan," she greeted me with a knowing smile. "I was wondering when you'd come by."

Her familiarity caught me completely off guard. "I'm sorry, but do we know each other?"

"Word gets around in a town like this," she said with a gentle laugh. "And I make it my business to know what's happening, especially when it involves magic."

I nodded, feeling slightly out of my depth. "I'm trying to understand the magic at Rewind Rentals. It's become a bit of a mystery, and I was hoping you could shed some light on it."

Lillian gestured for me to follow her to a small sitting area at the back of the shop. "I'm surprised that Amelia isn't here with you."

"She's feeling overwhelmed by all the attention the shop is getting," I said nervously. "I just want to help her understand her heritage a bit more. So she can make a sound decision with all the facts laid before her."

"Amelia's grandparents were quite special, you know. They were close friends of mine," Lillian said.

I tried not to show my skepticism. There was no way Lillian was a day over thirty.

She continued. "They had a deep connection with the magic that flows through Coral Cove. The projector you have was enchanted by them, a gift to keep the town's magic alive."

"But if that's true, why did they stop using it?" I asked, eager for answers.

"They didn't stop out of fear," Lillian explained. "They stopped because they were worried about the attention it was drawing. Not everyone sees magic as a gift. Some see it as something to be exploited."

I frowned, the weight of her words sinking in. "So, the objects appearing in the store... they're manifestations of the films?"

Lillian nodded. "Yes, and more. They're a reflection of the town's history, its stories coming to life. The magic preserves the heritage of Coral Cove, to remind people of the wonders that lie beneath the surface."

I sat back, absorbing the enormity of what she was saying. "And what should we do with this information?"

"Embrace it," Lillian said with a soft smile. "Use it to bring people together, to celebrate the uniqueness of Coral Cove. It's a legacy worth protecting."

Her words resonated with me, and I knew I had to share this revelation with Amelia. But first, I needed to tell my cousin, Rory. She was making a film about the store. I needed to give Amelia a real choice and a store worth fighting for.

I thanked Lillian for her time and insights, promising to keep her updated on our plans. This was no longer just about saving a store, it was about honoring a legacy, preserving the magic that made Coral Cove special.

Back at Rewind Rentals, I called Rory, eager to fill her in on everything I'd learned.

"Hey, Flynn," Rory answered, her voice bright with anticipation. "How's everything going?"

"You're not going to believe this," I said, launching into the story of my meeting with Lillian and the book from Park.

"Wow," she said, her voice tinged with awe. "That's incredible. We have to include this in the film."

"Exactly," I agreed. "I'll send you copies of everything I've found. This could really add depth to your project."

"Thanks, Flynn. I'm excited to see where this goes," Rory said.

"Can you help me with one other thing?" I asked.

"Anything."

After hanging up, I felt a renewed sense of determination. We were on the brink of something amazing, a beacon of magic and community. I'd only have to wait a little longer till I could tell Amelia.

NINE

Amelia

I n what felt like an instant, another week slipped away. Flynn and I were still tiptoeing around the beanbag sex.

I tried to focus on the task at hand, but my mind kept drifting back to the kiss we had shared. It was as if the memory of it had seared itself into my skin, every brush of his lips replaying in my mind. I could still feel the way his hands had gripped my waist, the way his breath had mingled with mine, the taste of him lingering on my lips.

The tension between us was palpable, even when we weren't touching. Flynn seemed to sense it too, his gaze following me whenever I moved, his body gravitating toward mine like a magnet. He was always just a little too close, his voice dropping to that low, intimate tone that made my insides flutter. I knew we needed to talk, to address what had happened, but the thought of it terrified me. What if he regretted it? What if he didn't feel the same way?

The uncertainty gnawed at me, making me short-tempered and distracted. But I couldn't bring myself to confront him, to risk shattering the fragile connection we had built. So, I avoided him, avoided being alone with him, even though every fiber of my being ached to be near him again. I knew I couldn't give him the attention he craved.

Besides, he made me wait six years. He could cool it for a couple of weeks.

Life at Rewind Theater and Rentals had found a new rhythm. The store was bustling, the movie nights were selling out, and we were constantly on our toes to keep up with the demand. The chaotic pace had become strangely comforting, a welcome distraction from the heavy decisions looming over me.

Last week, I overheard Flynn speaking quietly on a phone call. No matter what I did, that feeling stayed with me the entire week. I'd convinced myself he was accepting another job, and the anxiety gnawed at me. He was going to leave, again.

His voice was barely a whisper, but the few words I managed to catch sent a wave of dread crashing over me. "Yeah, I know it's a big opportunity... I'll consider it for sure... I'm just not sure if I'm ready to make a move. There's a lot at stake for me right now... Okay, I look forward to hearing from you again..."

I froze, my hand hovering over the doorknob. The conversation echoed with a seriousness that immediately sent my mind spiraling to the worst possible scenario.

Was Flynn actually considering leaving again?

Had he found another job that promised him everything he said he didn't want anymore?

Was I ever going to be enough?

I waited until the conversation ended before walking into the office, trying to act as casual as I could despite the knot tightening in my stomach.

"Who was that?" I asked, keeping my tone light.

Flynn looked up, his face unreadable. "Just... someone about an opportunity," he said, his eyes not quite meeting mine.

"What kind of opportunity?" I asked. My chest tightened as the weight of the unspoken goodbye settled in.

"Umm," he cleared his throat. "For me."

"Are you thinking about taking it?" I pressed, unable to keep the concern out of my voice.

He hesitated, and I could see him weighing his words. "I'm still thinking things over. Honestly, it doesn't matter."

Part of me wanted to push for more information, to demand to know what was going on in his head. Despite my inner conflict, I restrained myself. If he wanted to leave, he knew where the door was.

I forced a smile and nodded. "Okay, well, let me know if you need to talk about it."

"Of course," he said, offering a smile that didn't quite reach his eyes.

After overhearing Flynn's phone call, a sharp pang of jealousy and fear gripped my heart. The idea of him leaving again, of walking out of my life just when I was starting to let him back in, was unbearable. The thought consumed me, making me even more aware of the tension between us.

That evening, when we finally had a moment alone, the air was thick with unspoken words. Flynn stood close, too close, his hand brushing against mine as we talked. The contact sent a jolt through me, and I could feel the heat radiating off his body, drawing me in.

"Amelia," Flynn murmured, his voice low, almost a whisper. He stepped closer, his chest brushing against mine, his breath warm on my skin. "We need to talk."

My heart raced, and I knew we were standing on the edge of something irreversible. But before I could respond, his hand found my waist, pulling me closer until our bodies were pressed together. I could feel the hard planes of his chest against me, the tension in his muscles as he held himself back.

"Flynn," I breathed, my voice trembling with the weight of everything I wanted to say.

But before I could say another word, he kissed me again, hard and desperate, as if he were afraid this might be our last chance. The kiss was a storm, wild and untamed, and I surrendered to it, letting the waves of desire crash over me. We were both on fire, consumed by the heat that had been building between us for weeks.

I pulled away first, the sudden distance between us feeling like a cold shock. I cleared my throat, running a hand down my shirt as if smoothing out the fabric could also smooth out the feelings churning inside me. I took a step backward, creating a necessary physical barrier. Without meeting his eyes, I spun around and busied myself with the nearest task, anything to distract from the moment that had just passed between us.

The rest of the day passed in a blur of customer interactions and managing logistics, but Flynn's evasiveness lingered in the back of my mind. I couldn't shake the feeling that something was going on, something that he wasn't telling me. Conflicting emotions bubbled and resurfaced. I didn't enjoy any part of it.

As the week drew to a close, I found myself more and more excited about the upcoming grand reopening. The renovations were almost complete, and the store had undergone a stunning transformation. The theater was a hit, the profits were better than I could have ever imagined, and everything seemed to fall into place.

Despite the success, the question of whether to sell the store loomed. David Reed's offer was still on the table, and while I had decided not to worry about it until after the reopening, it was hard to ignore the financial security it promised.

Even with the tension, the reality was Flynn had been a rock through all of it. From helping me make minor changes and tweaks to optimize the store's operations, he had a knack for spotting what worked and what didn't, and his suggestions were invaluable.

As we ushered the last customer out and locked up for the night, Flynn turned to me with a mischievous grin. "I have a surprise for you."

"A surprise?" I asked, raising an eyebrow. "What kind of surprise?"

"Something special. I wanted to wait until after everyone's gone home and we're all locked up. I want to show you a film. It's something I think you'll really appreciate."

A flutter of excitement moved through me, and I followed him upstairs. "This isn't going to be a repeat of last time, is it?" I teased, trying to keep things light.

Flynn chuckled, a warm, genuine sound. "Would that be so bad?"

Heat pooled in my center at the memory, reminding me of all the feelings I still had for Flynn. Feelings I needed to sort out. "Okay, show me this surprise of yours."

The lights dimmed, and the only sound was the hum of the old projector.

"I promise this is something you'll want to see."

The film began, and the opening scenes immediately captivated me. It was Rory's documentary, featuring Rewind Rentals, its history, and the magic that had become part of its identity. The footage was beautifully shot, interwoven with stories about the town and its unique charm.

As I watched, a whirlwind of emotions stirred deep within me, my heart expanding. There were interviews with locals, tales of the magical events that had taken place, and glimpses into a past I hadn't known about. It was a love letter to the store, to my family, and to Coral Cove itself.

Flynn sat beside me, his presence reassuring. As the film continued, I realized what he had done. He had preserved part of my history forever, ensuring that the legacy of Rewind

Rentals would be known to the world no matter what decision I made.

Tears filled my eyes as the credits rolled. I turned to Flynn, overwhelmed by the gratitude I felt. "This is incredible. Flynn, I don't even know what to say."

He took my hand, his eyes soft and earnest. "No matter what you decide, Amelia, whether you sell the store or keep it, what you've made here will always be preserved. Several film circuits picked the documentary up, and people will know about Rewind Rentals and its magic."

I was at a loss for words, happiness and disbelief mingling in my chest. But the joy was tempered by the lingering doubt about the phone call I'd overheard more than a week ago. I had to know the truth.

I took a deep breath. "Flynn," I started.

He met my eyes.

"I overheard you talking on the phone about a job. Are you leaving?" My voice trembled as I asked, feeling the weight of it in every word.

He looked at me, his expression one of surprise, before a flash of understanding crossed it. "No, Amelia, I'm not going anywhere. I was talking to Rory. I wanted this to be a surprise, and I didn't want to spoil it. The film was the enormous opportunity we were talking about. She asked if you were still considering selling the store. I told her I didn't think you were ready to decide. That's all."

As the puzzle pieces fell into place, relief washed over me, and I felt foolish for doubting him. "So, you're not leaving?"

He shook his head. "I'm not leaving, Amelia. I'm here, and I'm staying."

"I'm sorry. I just… I've been so scared that you'd leave again."

He pulled me into his arms, holding me close. "You have nothing to be sorry for, Amelia. I understand where your fear is coming from. It's okay, I'm not leaving. I'm here for the long haul. I love you, and I want to be with you, Amelia Bennet."

Tears slipped down my cheeks. "I love you too, Flynn. I want to give us another chance. A real one."

He smiled, brushing the tears from my face, and kissed me with a tenderness that made my heart flutter.

The plush seat surrounded us in a cocoon of intimacy. The air seemed to crackle with anticipation as Flynn leaned in, his lips meeting mine in a lingering kiss. His touch was soft at first, exploring and teasing, until a spark of hunger ignited between us.

Eagerly, I threaded my hands through his hair, drawing him closer. The world outside ceased to exist. There was only Flynn. His presence was a heady mix of desire.

Our kiss deepened. Flynn's hands explored every inch of my body, discovering all the secret spots that would make me quiver with delight. He broke away, his warm breath caressing my skin as he whispered. "I've been thinking about this for weeks."

My pulse quickened at the promise in his voice. "Then stop thinking," I whispered.

His chuckle was low and wicked. Flynn kissed me again, more insistent this time. The air was thick with tension, a tangible force pulling us closer together.

Flynn's hands moved to my waist, lifting me effortlessly onto his lap. As I straddled him, my knees on either side of his hips, I could feel the undeniable presence of his erection pressing against me. It made my breath catch in my chest.

He pulled back slightly, eyes dark with need as he gazed into mine. His voice grew deeper as he murmured, "You're beautiful."

A flush of heat spread through me at his words. I reached for the hem of my shirt, tugging it over my head and tossing it aside. Flynn's eyes drank me in, his hands skimming over my bare skin with a touch that made me shiver.

His lips followed, trailing kisses along my neck and collarbone, each one a promise of the pleasure to come. I arched into him, my body aching for more of his touch.

With a playful grin, Flynn leaned back, his hands moving to my hips as he guided my movements. I gasped as he rocked me against him, feeling the evidence of his arousal pressing against my center.

"Flynn," I breathed, my voice dripping with desperate need and longing.

He responded with a soft groan, his hands tightening their grip on my hips as he pulled me closer. "I want to taste you," he said, his voice thick with desire.

I licked my lips, nodding as my body trembled with excitement. Flynn's gaze held mine as he gently shifted me off of his lap, helping me to stand. He knelt before me, his hands sliding down my sides, fingers curling around the waistband of my jeans.

I watched, captivated, as he slowly undid the button and slid the zipper down, his eyes never leaving mine. There was something deliciously wicked about the way he looked at me. It was a promise.

With a deft motion, Flynn eased my jeans down, leaving me exposed to his gaze. His hands lingered on my hips as he pressed a soft kiss to my stomach, warmth pooling in my belly.

I let out a soft moan, my fingers tangling in his hair as I guided him lower. Flynn obliged, his kisses trailing down my thighs, each touch setting my skin on fire.

Flynn paused, looking up at me with a devilish grin that made my heart skip a beat. Then, with deliberate slowness, he leaned in, his mouth a source of exquisite pleasure as he tasted me, his tongue tracing patterns on my clit that made my toes curl and my mind lose all focus.

My world narrowed to this moment, the sensation of Flynn's touch driving me to the edge of madness. My fingers tightened in his hair, urging him on as my body moved with a will of its own, lost in the ecstasy he gave me.

The first wave of pleasure crashed over me, and I cried out, body shuddering as Flynn continued his relentless assault, drawing out every last ounce of sensation until I was left breathless and trembling.

When I finally opened my eyes, Flynn was watching me, a satisfied smile playing on his lips. His voice, heavy with desire, whispered, "You taste even better than I remembered."

I laughed softly, pulling him up to me for a searing kiss, tasting myself on his tongue. My fingers worked at his belt, eager to free him from the confines of his clothes. Flynn helped, shrugging out of his shirt and jeans, and soon we were skin against skin, the heat of our bodies mingling in a dance of passion.

Flynn sank back into the seat, and I straddled him once more, my heart pounding with anticipation. I took him in, inch by inch, savoring the feel of him filling me completely.

Once he filled my core, we moved slowly, a languid rhythm that built with each heartbeat. My breath came in soft pants as I rode his exquisite cock, my body moving in time with his, our connection a symphony of shared desire.

Flynn's hands gripped my hips, guiding my movements with skill. The tension inside me built, a tightening coil of sensation that threatened to unravel at any moment.

"Flynn," I breathed, my voice a plea for release.

He responded with a soft groan—his eyes darkening with desire. With a sudden burst of energy, he flipped me onto my back, my body cradled by the plush seat as he thrust into me with a newfound urgency.

I cried out, my senses overwhelmed by the intensity of his movement. Flynn's hands were everywhere, tracing patterns on my skin, his mouth claiming mine in a kiss that spoke of possession and love.

The world around us faded to nothing, leaving only the

two of us entwined in this intimate dance. His thick, hard shaft thrusting inside of me, the feel of his body moving in time with my own, drove me to the brink, and I surrendered to the pleasure that washed over me in waves.

Like a sudden storm, the climax engulfed me with intensity. I couldn't control the shudders that ran through my body as he held me, and all I could do was call out his name. Flynn followed soon after, his own release, a powerful surge, leaving him breathless.

We lay together, wrapped in the aftermath of our shared passion, the theater a silent witness to the bond we'd forged. I rested my head against Flynn's chest, listening to the steady beat of his heart as I savored the warmth of his embrace.

With all inhibitions abandoned, we made love again, our hearts open and our emotions unleashed. It was better than before, a connection that felt right and true. In this moment, I knew without a doubt that this was where I belonged—in the arms of the man I loved, in the sanctuary of our shared world.

TEN

T he excitement in Coral Cove was palpable as word spread that the documentary featuring Rewind Rentals had been accepted into several film festivals. The phone hadn't stopped ringing for days, with journalists, bloggers, and film enthusiasts eager to know more about the magical rental store that had captured the hearts of so many.

It was surreal to think that our little slice of nostalgia was making such waves. I couldn't help but smile every time I saw the look of pride on Amelia's face as she read through the emails and social media comments, praising her dedication and vision.

"Flynn, can you believe this?" Amelia said one afternoon, her eyes wide with disbelief as she scanned through the latest message on her phone. I kissed her neck. "I've been invited to present at the Coastal Film Festival next month!"

I grinned, my chest swelling with pride. "You deserve this, Amelia. You and Rewind Rentals both. This is your legacy, and it's finally getting the recognition it deserves."

She looked up at me, her expression softening. "I couldn't have done any of this without you, you know. Your support and belief in this place have meant everything to me."

I reached across the counter and squeezed her hand, feeling the warmth of her touch. "We make a pretty great team, don't we?"

Her smile was answer enough, and it filled me with a sense of contentment that I hadn't felt in years.

As the buzz around the documentary continued to grow, we threw ourselves into planning the grand reopening event for the store. It was the perfect opportunity to unveil the film to the community and celebrate the transformation of Rewind Rentals into a beloved local attraction and tourist destination.

The preparations were intense. We wanted everything to be perfect—the decorations, the refreshments, the screenings —and we worked tirelessly to ensure that the event would be a memorable one.

Amelia and I spent hours in the theater room, tweaking the seating arrangement and testing the sound system to make sure it was just right. We organized a lineup of classic films to be shown throughout the reopening day for free, interspersed with clips from the documentary.

"I think we're ready," Amelia said, stepping back to admire our handiwork. "The place looks incredible."

I nodded, taking in the newly polished floors, the vintage posters lining the walls, and the cozy seating area that had become the heart of Rewind Rentals. "It really does. You've created something amazing here."

The night of the grand reopening arrived, and the store was buzzing with anticipation. The line stretched down the block, a mix of folks eager to experience the magic of The Rewind Theater.

As the doors opened and the crowd poured in, I watched with a sense of pride as Amelia greeted guests, her energy infectious. The documentary played on a loop in the rental shop downstairs and upstairs between showings. It drew in a lot of "oohs" and "ahhs" from the audience as they marveled at the story of our store and its mystical legacy.

The event was a resounding success. People laughed, reminisced, and shared stories of their own experiences with movies and magic. By the end of the night, Rewind Rentals had cemented itself as a cherished part of Coral Cove, a place where memories were made and dreams came to life.

As the last of the guests trickled out, Amelia and I sat together on one of the theater couches, exhaustion mingling with satisfaction.

"We did it," I said, wrapping an arm around her shoulders. "Rewind Rentals is officially the hottest spot in Coral Cove."

Amelia leaned into me, her head resting on my chest. "I can hardly believe it. It feels like a dream."

"It's real," I assured her. "And it's all because of you."

She lifted her head, her eyes meeting mine with a mixture of gratitude and love. "Flynn, I don't think I've ever been happier."

"Does this mean you're not going to sell?" I asked.

"I already called to tell him thanks, but no thanks."

Relief washed over me. "I'm glad to hear it," I said, my heart pounding as I prepared to take the next step. "Because there's something I want to ask you."

Amelia sat up, curiosity sparkling in her eyes. "What is it?"

Taking a deep breath, I reached into my pocket and pulled out a small box, feeling a wave of nerves crash over me. "I know we've been through a lot, and we've worked so hard to get here, but I can't imagine spending another day without you by my side. Amelia Bennet, will you be my partner—not just in business, but in life?" I opened the box to reveal a morganite ring. "Will you marry me?"

I watched as her eyes widened in surprise, and my heart skipped a beat, fearing I had pushed her too soon. But in an instant, her expression transformed into a beaming smile, and she enthusiastically wrapped her arms around me, almost causing us to tumble from the couch.

"Yes!" she exclaimed, laughter bubbling up from her chest. "Yes, Flynn, a thousand times, yes!"

Relief and joy flooded through me as I kissed her, feeling the last of my doubts melt away. We were in this together, now and forever.

Epilogue

AMELIA

T he sun set over Coral Cove, casting a warm, golden hue that danced across the waters and painted the sky in shades of pink and orange. Standing at the entrance of Rewind Rentals, I took a deep breath, savoring the sweet smell of popcorn and the sound of laughter that drifted from inside the store. The grand reopening had been everything I could have hoped for, and more.

In the weeks that followed, the buzz from the documentary continued to grow. It had not only been accepted into multiple film festivals, but it also won awards, garnering attention far beyond what we had imagined. Each award brought a new wave of visitors, eager to experience the magic of The Rewind Theater for themselves. The store had become a cultural landmark, offering not just movie rentals, but a nostalgic and enchanting experience that resonated with people from all walks of life.

Flynn and I were amazed by the response, and as our days grew busier, our relationship blossomed alongside the success of our store—a seamless intertwining of our lives. The magic of Coral Cove had found its home in Rewind Rentals, and we embraced it wholeheartedly, hosting special events that celebrated the town's unique history and enchantment.

We expanded our business model, collaborating with other local shops and artists to create a vibrant community hub. These partnerships breathed new life into the store, attracting an even broader audience and making Rewind Rentals a centerpiece of the community. We even planned to turn the third and fourth floors into additional theaters in time.

I walked to the counter, where my parents stood, their faces beaming with pride as they watched the bustling store. It was a busy Saturday afternoon, and every corner of the store was filled with life—families picking out movies, couples holding hands as they browsed, and groups of friends laughing as they reminisced about old film favorites.

"You've done us proud, Amelia," my mother said, clapping me on the back. "Your grandparents would be overjoyed to witness the amazing things you have achieved."

Tears shimmered in my eyes, and I hugged them both tightly. "Thank you. I couldn't have done it without you," I said, feeling the familiar warmth of love and gratitude wash over me.

As the evening drew on and the crowd thinned, I found myself at the counter, watching the store buzz. I felt a deep sense of fulfillment and purpose, knowing that Rewind Rentals was more than just a business; it was a testament to what could be achieved when people came together with a shared dream.

Flynn joined me, slipping his hand into mine, his presence grounding and reassuring. "What are you thinking about?" he asked.

"Just how far we've come," I replied, squeezing his hand. "And how grateful I am for all of it."

He smiled, the kind of smile that reached his eyes and

made my heart skip a beat. "I'm grateful too. We make a pretty good team, don't we?"

"The best," I agreed, feeling the truth of it resonate in my bones.

Together, we stood there, savoring the moment as the store hummed around us, creating a comforting symphony. It served as a powerful reminder of how community, love, and the invisible threads of magic intertwined to create something truly remarkable.

As the night settled over Coral Cove, I knew that whatever the future held, we would face it side by side. The magic of this town had woven its spell around us, and I was more than happy to be caught in its enchanting embrace.

Rewind Rentals would always be a place of wonder and nostalgia, a beacon of magic in Coral Cove. And as Flynn wrapped his arm around me, pulling me close, I felt a profound sense of peace and joy.

"This is where we belong," I said softly, leaning into him.

Flynn nodded, his gaze warm and full of love. "This is our home, Amelia. It's our story."

* * *

Sign up for Jax Wilder's newsletter and receive a collection of unpublished Coral Cove short stories. Meet familiar characters and dive deeper into the love and romance that Coral Cove is known for. Don't miss out on this exclusive content!

If you enjoyed Love Rewound, you'll want to check out
Amelia and Flynn's story in the
Tarot Fantasies series

Six of Cups

Some love stories need to be rewound
to be truly understood.

Amelia:

I'm haunted by memories of my first love, Flynn. Can revisiting the past help me finally move on, or will it pull me back into the love I've never fully let go of?

Flynn:

Amelia always saw the best in me, even when I couldn't. Now, I'm back in her life, but only as a memory. Can I help her heal, or will our past keep haunting us both?

In the mystical heart of the Arcane Room, where memories come alive and the past intertwines with the present, Amelia is on a quest for closure. Haunted by the lingering emotions of her first love, she returns to the enigmatic room to confront the memories that have held her captive for years. But as the past unfurls before her eyes, she discovers that some memories are more powerful—and more painful—than she ever imagined.

Guided by the Six of Cups tarot card, a symbol of nostalgia and childhood innocence, Amelia is drawn into a world where the lines between reality and fantasy blur. Each memory brings her closer to the truth about her relationship with Flynn, forcing her to face the joys and sorrows of their love story.

As the memories unfold, Amelia must decide if she's ready to finally let go of the past or if she'll be forever bound by the love she lost. In this emotionally charged journey, "Six of Cups" weaves a tale of love, loss, and the enduring power of memories.

Perfect for fans of romantic fantasy, magical realism, and emotional journeys of self-discovery, "Six of Cups" will take you on a heart-wrenching ride through the most cherished and painful moments of a love that was never meant to be forgotten.

Also by Jax Wilder

<u>Coral Cove Series</u>

Sleighed by Love

Harvesting Love

Dawning Desire

Knead You Now

Haunted by Her

Perfect Lover Spell

Love Rewound

<u>Tarot Fantasies Series:</u>

The Devil's Temptations

Strength of the Beast

Hanged Passions

Six of Cups

Death's Embrace

Three of Swords

Jax Wilder

Additional Titles From

Rainbow Quartz Publishing

Miranda Levi

From A Youth A Fountain Did Flow

The Sea Withdrew

A Tear In Time

Mo(ther) Na(ture)

In Orion's Hands

Jackson Anhalt

From The 911 Files

Lorelai Hamilton

Find Your Bliss

Teenage Witch's Grimoire

Tarot Reflection Journal

Tarot Refection Journal Coloring The Tarot

The Eclectic Witch's Grimoire

Dream Journal

Teenage Tarot

Tarot Tales and Magic Spells

Arcane In Verse

Isla Watts

A Fairy Bad Day

Surprise! You're a Vampire

Gorgeous, Gorgeous, Gorgons

Mork The Handsome Orc

Adopted By Werewolves

Bite Me If You Can

That's The Spirit!

Rose Dawson's Book Journals:

My Time With The Fairies

Enchanted Escapades

Enchanted Escapades

Dewey Decimal Diaries

Siren's Songbook

Pride and Prejudice

Bibliophile's Bounty

Book of Books Journal

Pages & Passages Reading Journal

Bookworm's Companion Reading Journal & Tracker

About the Author

Jax Wilder is a passionate romance author hailing from a charming small town nestled in the picturesque Pacific Northwest. With a heart full of love and an unyielding belief in the power of happily ever afters, Jax weaves enchanting tales of love and connection that leave readers captivated.

Jax's novels are a reflection of her commitment to celebrating the magic of love, and her characters' journeys mirror the warmth and happiness she has found in her own life. Join her on the enchanting journey of love, passion, and enduring connection through her heartfelt romance novels.

amazon.com/stores/Jax-Wilder/author/B0CM36CSH1?ref=ap_r-dr&isDramIntegrated=true&shoppingPortalEnabled=true